Henry and Mudge
UNDER THE
Yellow Moon

The Fourth Book of Their Adventures

Story by Cynthia Rylant
Pictures by Suçie Stevenson

A TRUMPET CLUB SPECIAL EDITION

For Tony Manna
and Rebecca Cross — CR

For Jane — SS

Published by The Trumpet Club
666 Fifth Avenue, New York, New York 10103

ISBN: 0-440-84462-2

This edition published by arrangement with Bradbury Press,
an affiliate of Macmillan Publishing Company
Printed in the United States of America

September 1991

The text of this book is set in 18 pt. Goudy Old Style.
The illustrations are watercolor and reproduced in full color.
Book design by Mina Greenstein

10 9 8 7 6 5 4 3 2 1
UPC

Contents

Together in the Fall

In the fall,
Henry and his big dog Mudge
took long walks in the woods.

5

Henry loved looking at
the tops of the trees.
He liked the leaves:
orange, yellow, brown, and red.

Mudge loved sniffing at the ground.

And he liked the leaves, too.

He always ate a few.

In the fall,
Henry liked counting the birds
flying south.
Mudge liked
watching for busy chipmunks.

Since one was a boy
and the other was a dog,
they never did things
just the same way.

Henry picked apples
and Mudge licked apples.

Henry put on a coat
and Mudge grew one.
And when the fall wind blew,
Henry's ears turned red
and Mudge's ears
turned inside out.

But one thing about them
was the same.
In the fall
Henry and Mudge liked
being together,
most of all.

Under the
Yellow Moon

Henry loved Halloween.
He loved to make
jack-o'-lanterns.
He loved to make
paper bats.

And most of all
he loved to dress up.

But there was one thing about Halloween
Henry did not like:
ghost stories.
And Henry's mother
loved to tell ghost stories.

Every Halloween
she put on her witch's hat,
lit candles,
and told ghost stories.

She thought Henry liked them
because he told her
he liked them.

But really he hated them.
They scared him.
He was afraid to tell her that.

But this year Henry had Mudge.
Mudge would be with him.
Henry would not be afraid
of the ghost stories.

So Halloween night
Henry's mother put on her hat
and lit her candles.

She invited Henry and Mudge
and some of Henry's friends
to listen to ghost stories.

It was dark outside.

A big yellow moon was in the sky.

It was dark inside,

except for the candles

and one jack-o'-lantern.

Henry got close to Mudge

on the floor.

Henry's mother began.

First she told a story
about a man who lost his head.
Henry shook.
His friends shook.

Then she told a story
about a cat in a graveyard.
The candles made shapes on the walls.
Henry shook harder.

Then Henry's mother
began telling a story
about a pair of shoes
that went looking for
someone's feet.

The shoes, she said,
came out only at night.
And they walked up and down
the streets, looking.

"You could hear them,"
she said softly.
"They went CLICK . . . CLICK . . .
CLICK . . . CLICK."
Henry's mother tapped
her own shoes on the floor.

"CLICK . . . CLICK . . . CLICK,"
she whispered.

But when she stopped tapping,
Henry still heard something.
Something in the room.
Something in the room
under the yellow moon.
Henry held his breath.

Something went
CLICK . . . CLICK . . .
CLICK . . . CLICK.
But faster.

Henry's whole body shook.
It was like someone walking
faster and faster.
CLICK-CLICK-CLICK-CLICK-
CLICK-CLICK.
What was it?

Henry's mother bent down.

"Mudge?" she said.

Henry knew his mother was scared, too,

if she needed Mudge.

"Mudge?" she said again.

The clicking got louder.

The shoes are coming! thought Henry.

He put his head in Mudge's neck.

Now the clicking was louder than ever.

30

"Mudge," Henry's mother said,
"stop chattering."

Chattering?
Henry put his ear
near Mudge's mouth.
And Mudge's teeth went
CLICK-CLICK-CLICK-CLICK-
CLICK-CLICK.

It wasn't a pair of shoes!
It was Mudge!
And he was more scared
of the yellow moon
and the dark room
and the witch's stories
than anybody else!
Poor Mudge, thought Henry.
Henry stopped shaking
and put his arms
around Mudge's big head
and held Mudge tight.

Then they listened
to the next story
about a chair that rocked
all by itself.
But Mudge clicked
all the way to the end.

Thanksgiving Guest

In November,
Henry's Aunt Sally always came.
She came one week
before Thanksgiving.

She left one week
after Thanksgiving.
That is why Henry
did not like Thanksgiving.
Because Henry did not like
Aunt Sally.

She talks too much,
Henry thought.

She eats too much,
Henry thought.
She hogs the TV,
Henry thought.
Henry wished Aunt Sally
would stay home.

Aunt Sally had not yet
seen Henry's dog Mudge.
I bet she hates dogs,
Henry thought.
Oh, how he wished
Aunt Sally would stay home.
But she didn't.

She came one week
before Thanksgiving,
right on time.
Aunt Sally came
into Henry's house.

She was
talking and talking and talking.
She went right
into the kitchen
with Henry's father.

Henry knew what
Aunt Sally would be
doing in the kitchen.
Henry went in the backyard
to find Mudge.
At last, Henry thought that
Aunt Sally must be finished
talking and eating.
So he went back inside
with Mudge.

They walked into the kitchen.

Aunt Sally was still eating.

"*Good grief!*" she yelled.

Henry and Mudge stepped back.

I knew she'd hate dogs,
Henry thought.
Aunt Sally looked at Mudge.
"Good grief!" she said again.

But then,

she took a cracker

off her plate.

She threw it to Mudge.

SNAP! went Mudge's mouth.

And the cracker was gone.

Henry looked at Mudge.

Henry looked at Aunt Sally.

"Great dog," Aunt Sally said.

She put a cracker in her own mouth.

"Want one?" she asked Henry.

"Sure," said Henry.

He sat down with Aunt Sally.

She still ate too much.

She still talked too much.

But all of her talk

this time was about Mudge.

And *that* was different.

Aunt Sally talked about

Mudge's sweet eyes.

She talked about

Mudge's strong chest.

She talked about

Mudge's soft fur.

She talked about

Mudge's good manners.

And she fed Mudge
lots of crackers.

This year, Henry knew,
he was going to
like Thanksgiving.
This year, Henry knew,
he really had something
to be thankful for!